Where the Four Winds Blow

Dan Yaccarino

JOANNA COTLER BOOKS

An Imprint of HarperCollins*Publishers*

Library of Congress Cataloging-in-Publication Data

Yaccarino, Dan.

Where the Four Winds blow / Dan Yaccarino.— 1st ed.

    p.   cm.

Summary: Upset that his busy parents ignore him, Roger wishes they would be blown away, but
then he and his irritable sister must endure a fantastic journey in order to find them.

ISBN 0-06-623626-6 — ISBN 0-06-623627-4 (lib. bdg.)

[1. Family life—Fiction.   2. Brothers and sisters—Fiction.   3. Weather—Fiction.]   I. Title.

PZ7.Y125 Wh   2003   2002001327

[Fic]—dc21

Typography by Alicia Mikles

1 2 3 4 5 6 7 8 9 10

❖

First Edition

For Lucia Rose

Chapter One

A gentle breeze blew through Roger's bedroom, upsetting his many papers. "Darn," he said as he closed the window. His room was the only place he could be safe from his annoying older sister, Sally. When she wasn't calling him Fathead and making his life miserable, she was talking on her phone, brushing her hair, or shopping at the mall with Mom's credit card. Roger couldn't stand her.

His room was filled with charts, diagrams, and a globe. Roger was fascinated with anything to do with science, his favorite topic being the weather. He spent his time building models, watching the Science Channel on television, and staring out his window daydreaming for hours.

Once, when he'd told Sally he'd like to be a meteorologist and chart weather patterns, she'd laughed and reminded him that whenever there was a thunderstorm he hid under his bed. "You're a big baby! What are you going to do if you're at work and there's a storm? Hide under your desk?"

An argument erupted. Roger called to Mom for support, but she'd been busy on the phone arranging another social club party, fingernail appointment, or whatever. "Now, Sweetie," Mom had said, "stop arguing with your sister! Can't you see I'm busy?"

Dad, however, was almost never home. When he was, he would be in his study working or talking on the telephone anyway. So whenever Roger and Sally fought—which was often—their dad automatically scolded Roger, even if it wasn't his fault. Which it never was.

"Hey there, Coach," Dad would say, "you know better than to fight with a girl."

It didn't seem to matter to Dad that even though Sally was a girl, she still was a head taller than Roger and beat him up every chance she got. As long as no one was looking, that is.

The only things Roger's parents did together was go to cocktail parties and play golf or tennis at the club. When they did see each other, they acted so ridiculous. Roger found it especially nauseating when his mother called his dad Sweetie Pie and Pookums and other stupid names.

Last summer, they had sent Roger to soccer camp. He wasn't allowed to watch television, the food stunk, and all they did was play soccer. He begged them not to make him go, but Mom and Dad sent him anyway. They were going to Europe for six weeks and couldn't leave Roger and Sally alone.

"It's not like you're around much anyway," Roger protested.

He got punished for that, but later his dad bought him a train set. Not that that made up for anything—it stayed in the box.

But he was pretty happy now that school was over, there was no camp, and he had the summer to dedicate to scientific pursuits. Roger actually used to like school, but that was last year at his old school in his old neighborhood. Everything changed when Dad got a promotion. Roger and his family had moved into a new house in a new neighborhood, where Roger hadn't cared much for anything but staying in and conducting experiments from a book he found, *Fun with Science*. Everything he needed was right there in his bedroom. That was just how he liked it and he preferred not to leave.

The outdoors, he thought, was highly overrated.

On some weekends, the family had dinner together—well, sort of. They all sat at the dinner table, eating some strange cuisine Mom had ordered in or prepared, but they never said a word to one another. That's not to say it was quiet, because it wasn't. Dad would be on the phone with clients in the Far East, Mom would be watching the latest celebrity chef on her mini TV, Sally would be blasting her music, and Roger would be playing an obnoxiously loud video game. You couldn't hear yourself crunch on your batter-fried octopus legs, poached quail eggs, or whatever Mom had seen on television that week and thought they "simply must try."

"Mom?" Roger had once asked.

"Gwendoline. Remember, dear, call Mommy by her first name," Mom had said.

"Uh, Gwendoline, why don't you just cook regular food? You know, like hamburgers or barbecued chicken or something?"

She'd looked at Roger as if she were smelling a dead fish. "Honey," Mom had answered, "we don't have to eat that anymore."

On the nights Mom and Dad weren't home, Mom left little notes taped to the microwave with directions on heating the frozen dinners, or a pile of menus from restaurants that delivered. In fact, Roger ordered in so often, the deliverymen not only knew him by name but knew that he liked extra cheese on his pizza and his Szechuan chicken and cashews without the cashews. Mom also left lists of reasons why she wouldn't be home until way past his bedtime, so he'd better be in bed when she did.

The house they lived in was big. Well,

bigger than the house Roger lived in for his first eight years. He'd had to share a bedroom with his sister then. Now she had her own room, with a phone no less, and he had become Fathead.

If there was one thing Mom and Dad loved to do more than talk on their phones, go to cocktail parties, and call each other silly names, it was to give presents. On birthdays or Christmas, Roger would get catcher's mitts, hockey masks, and footballs.

"But I don't like sports, Dad."

It didn't matter.

"Hey there, Tiger, every boy should play sports."

And then, like clock-work, came the story of how Dad had been captain of both the football and basket-ball teams at once.

Sally always got what she wanted—clothes. She could never have enough. Roger never got what he wanted but tried his best with what he received. When he had accumulated enough tennis, soccer, and golf balls, he made a model of the solar system with a basketball as the sun.

The wind was getting stronger outside, but Roger was glued to his favorite television show, *Wonders of Science*. During a commercial for a state-of-the-art telescope, Roger decided he had to have it, immediately. He went to Mom and begged her to buy it for him. As usual, she was on the phone gossiping, planning a luau, or recommending caterers.

"Mom, I want the telescope on TV," Roger said.

"Pumpkin, now what did I tell you?" she asked a little crossly.

"Gwendoline." Roger sighed. "I want the telescope on TV."

"No! I told you never to interrupt Mommy

when she's on the telephone!" she answered sharply, wagging her perfectly manicured finger at him.

Roger shuffled away, grumbling to himself.

He walked into Dad's study to make his case but, big surprise, Dad was also talking on the phone. He sounded mad at the guy on the other end, but Roger interrupted him anyway.

"How many times do I have to tell you, Sport, when I'm in here, you can't pester me!" he roared at Roger, and went back to roaring at the man on the phone. Roger left, muttering that it never used to be like this.

A big storm was threatening to blow through town, and when Roger got back to his room, Sally was there to tease him.

"Big storm coming! You better make sure you tell Mom to tuck you in under your bed tonight!" She laughed as she walked to her room.

Roger didn't think it was at all funny.

He was ready for the storm: flashlight, stopwatch, and barometer on hand. He could hear the far-off low thunder and see dim flashes of lightning reflected on the ceiling.

Must be at least ten miles away, he thought. Roger calculated this by the amount of time between the lightning flash and thunderclap.

Boom, went the thunder. *Boom! Boom! Clap!* It was a lot closer now, about four miles away, Roger figured. Then came the worst part of all. The wind. Roger was curious about—but at the same time terrified by—the powerful wind that slammed the shutters against the house, spun the weather vane on the roof wildly, and made that scary howl through the attic.

Wooooo! wailed the wind.

As Roger lay in his bed listening to the storm, he became mad all over again.

Ka-thunk, ka-thunk, ka-thunk. A branch of the old oak tree slammed against the side of the house.

Roger thought about how his parents ignored his requests for the telescope.

KA-BOOM! hollered the thunder.

In fact, they never listened to anything he said at all.

CRA-ACK! cried a flash of lightning as it lit up his room.

Roger listened to the storm knock down trees, throw around patio furniture, and carry away garbage cans.

The more Roger thought about it, the angrier he became. Roger was so mad, he hopped out of his bed and threw open the window.

A huge gust of wind and rain blew through his room. Papers flew everywhere, his mobile spun around and around, and his globe toppled off his desk.

"I wish you'd carry Mom and Dad away, too!"

he shouted into the wind that was blowing in his face.

Then it stopped. Everything was quiet.

After a while, Roger could see faint flashes of lightning and hear the far-off rumble of thunder.

The storm had moved on.

All Roger heard was the rain falling on the roof.

Chapter Two

Bright yellow sunlight streaming through the window woke up Roger and made him blink. The house was strangely silent. After getting dressed, Roger crept downstairs to find no one there. Maybe Mom was at her tennis lesson and Dad was playing golf. No notes anywhere to tell him. He woke up Sally.

"Beat it, Fathead," she grumbled, and pulled the covers over her head.

After much pestering, he managed to get Sally out of bed. They looked in the yard, the garage, the basement—all the rooms in the house. They searched from top to bottom, but Mom and Dad were gone, that was for sure.

"Where could they be?" asked Sally.

"Maybe they went to Bermuda or Bora Bora or someplace and forgot to tell us."

"I hope Mom left her credit card," Sally said to herself.

They waited and waited, but Mom and Dad never came home or even telephoned. Roger decided to use the opportunity to finally conduct what he considered to be his most ground-breaking in a series of science experiments. He gathered up cleaning fluid, cold medicine, vegetable oil, and mysterious fluids from a chemistry set he had received in exchange for twenty-eight box tops from some lousy cereal that had been secretly flushed down the toilet.

He poured it all into the bathtub. The mixture turned from a putrid grayish pink to a deep purplish blue, then it bubbled and burped as if it were sort of angry. It smelled like rotten eggs and stinky feet. Roger left the bathroom window open all day and overnight to try to get rid of the awful smell. So much for brilliant advances in the field of bathroom science.

The next day, Roger cautiously peeked in the bathroom to check on his experiment, but the tub was empty. Had it run down the drain by itself, or had Sally unplugged the stopper? She insisted that she never touched "that gross stuff," but Roger knew she had to be lying. The mixture certainly couldn't have just slithered away on its own. Roger tried his best to forget about it.

After three days of eating cookies, wearing the same underwear, and staying up way past his bedtime, Roger had a suggestion. "Maybe we should go out and look for Mom and Dad." Sally finally agreed, but only because she was getting bored and wanted to get to the mall. Roger packed up some maps, charts, and his globe—just in case.

"On an expedition like this," he said, "you never can be too prepared."

On their way out the back door, Sally slipped and fell. She examined the bottom of her shoes. "Hey, Fathead, did you spill jam on the floor? You know, Mom's gonna kill you!"

Roger denied ever eating jam, but that strange purple color looked very familiar.

Roger decided not to say anything to Sally. Besides, they were on their way to find Mom and Dad.

Now, since they had no idea where to go, Sally and Roger decided to walk around their neighborhood. But before they got halfway down the driveway, they heard a strange voice.

"*Squawk*. Well, well, well, it's about time you figured out they weren't coming back."

Sally and Roger couldn't see where the voice was coming from. It spoke again.

"*Squawk*. I bet you have no idea where you're going, do you?"

"Who said that?" Sally demanded.

Up on the roof the weather vane grinned and flapped his wings.

"I didn't know you could talk," said Roger. He was more than a little surprised.

"Yeah, well, there's a lot of things you don't know, kid. *Squawk*. You should get out of the house more often. You too, girlie, and the mall doesn't count!"

The weather vane looked down on them as he slowly turned in the warm afternoon breeze.

"I bet you're looking for your parents, although I don't know why. Roger, you sure didn't want them around a few days ago, did you?"

"How did you know that?" Roger's heart fluttered. He dropped his globe and chased it down the driveway.

"Hey," exclaimed the weather vane, "you don't spin around on this roof as long as I have and not learn a few things. *Squawk.* What's the matter, honey, run out of hair ribbons?" The weather vane snickered at Sally.

"Shut up! Who asked you anyway, you crummy chicken!" she yelled.

"Keep that up, sister, and I won't tell you where they are."

Roger made his way back up the driveway and demanded that the rooster tell them what had happened to their parents.

"I'm gonna give you two a break. Not because I like you but because I hate the Four Winds," squawked the weather vane.

"You remember that big storm a few nights ago?" Roger nodded. "Well, the Four Wind brothers blew into town looking for trouble. *Hoo-wee!* They spun me around and around. I just hate it when they do that. Oh, they uprooted trees, downed power lines, and—"

"Get to the point," Sally said impatiently.

"Well," explained the weather vane, "they figured since you didn't want your parents anymore, Roger . . . didn't you wish they would be taken away?"

"You wished *that*?" Sally yelled, pushing Roger in the chest. "What are you—stupid?"

"Oh, yeah? I bet you sometimes wish they

would disappear, too," he said, defending himself.

"Yeah, but not until I get my driver's license, nitwit!"

They bickered back and forth for a while until, "Ahem," the weather vane interjected, as he folded his wings. "Do you want to know which way they went or not?"

Roger and Sally said they did and to make it snappy. He told them that the Four Winds could be found if they walked to the horizon and made a left at the setting sun.

"You can't miss 'em."

Roger scoffed at this. He explained that they could never reach the horizon because the earth is round.

"*Squawk.* That's what *you* think, Junior." The weather vane laughed, spinning faster now.

So Roger and Sally set off. They trudged out of their neighborhood, past the field where Roger's dad tried to teach him to play

baseball, past the trees and hills, past everything they knew.

They walked and walked and walked
toward the horizon and the setting sun,
arguing all the way.

Chapter Three

There it was—the horizon! Roger couldn't believe it. It dropped off into what looked like nowhere. Could his books and maps be wrong? Sally, exhausted, didn't seem to care very much. All she wanted to do was find Mom and Dad and get to the mall before it closed. The heat was unbearable as the setting sun lowered itself past them.

"Well, I'll be!" said the orangy Sun, who was quite surprised to see them there. "What're you kids doin' here? Go home! Git! This is no place fer younguns!" He chuckled.

"Quit your cackling, hayseed. We need directions," Sally yelled at him.

The Sun frowned. "I don't take kindly to that sort of attitude, Missy."

"Yeah, well, lump it, goober," she snapped
back.

The Sun frowned and radiated so much
heat, it made them sweat, and it hurt their
eyes. One of Roger's maps caught fire. He
threw it on the ground and stamped out the
flames.

"Okay, okay, we get the point." Roger surrendered. "Just tell us where to find the Four Winds and we'll be on our way."

"The Four Winds! What do you want with them no 'count ornery varmints for, anyway?" asked the Sun.

"They took our parents away," replied Roger.

"Are you sure yer folks didn't run away?" asked the Sun snidely.

"Listen, pal, could you cut the commentary and just point us in the right direction?" said Sally.

Roger shot Sally a look and then patiently explained to the Sun, "Someone told us that when we reached the horizon, we should make a left. But now we're not sure."

"Make a left? Whoever told you that certainly had no sense of direction a' tall!" commented the Sun, who was now anxious to get back to work and less anxious to talk to two rude little children.

"Hey," snapped Sally, "we didn't ask for

your opinion, we just want to know how to find the Four Winds."

"That's *it*. You can go chase yer shadows!" yelled the Sun.

With that, Sally's and Roger's shadows, which had been so obedient and reliable in pantomiming their every move, suddenly ran away. Sally and Roger ran as fast as they could to catch them, but the faster they went, the faster their shadows would go. Roger lost a few of his charts and a map in the chase, and to make matters worse, they were now approaching a huge, dark forest.

"Peee-yeeew!" Sally grimaced. "When was the last time you took a bath? Your feet *stink*!"

Roger stopped dead in his tracks, catching a faint whiff of the distinct odor of rotten eggs.

"Why did you stop? We're going to lose our shadows, you fathead! Come on!" yelled Sally.

"Wait," said Roger as he sniffed the breeze.

"It's here," he said, terrified.

"What's here?"

Roger explained about his experiment in the bathtub. Maybe the result had somehow managed to follow them.

"Well, I guess you finally did it," she said. "You lost your marbles."

Out of the corner of his eye, Roger could swear he saw a purple patch of ground on a hill off in the distance. *Could it be?* he thought. *Nah.*

"C'mon," Sally said. "Let's keep moving."

They still had their runaway shadows to catch, so they proceeded toward the forest. They were soon surrounded by tall, lush trees and gigantic bushes. The air was humid and sticky and felt like rain. It reminded Roger of a documentary about the rain forest he had seen on television.

Chapter Four

Sally and Roger crept through the damp forest still in pursuit of their shadows. There was no sign of them, and the more they walked, the more lost they got. They broke through vines and walked through deep green plants with leaves bigger than they were.

Sally spied her shadow, gentle and still, lying on a patch of wet leaves and dirt. She sneaked up and leaped on it. It tried to get away, but no such luck. That poor shadow was stuck to rotten little Sally forever. The tall trees rustled and Roger crept over, ready to pounce on his fugitive shadow just a few feet away.

"Who are you?" asked a soft voice with a Spanish accent from high above as Roger caught his shadow.

Roger and Sally looked up to see a beautiful woman, at least one hundred feet tall, with garlands of flowers for hair. Butterflies and chirping birds flew around her head. She held a massive umbrella under which drizzled rain.

"Hey, lady," Sally called up to her, "are you making it rain?" She could hardly see the woman's face.

"Why, yes," the lovely woman answered, sweetly looking down on them.

"Well, *quit* it!" screamed Sally. "You're ruining my dress!"

With that, the woman whipped up a downpour, and soon Sally and Roger were soaked to the skin.

"Now, what were you saying, my dear?"

"Never mind," Sally answered, her hair ribbon limp.

"Thanks a lot," said Roger as he wrung out his shirt.

The beautiful woman told them that she was the rain and that she and the Sun worked together in harmony to give life and make things grow. As she explained this, small colorful buds pushed their way through the wet ground where Sally and Roger stood and reached toward the sky.

"Oh, I know how rain happens," said Roger. "Scientifically speaking, most clouds are made up of tiny water droplets. Sometimes, as the air cools, these droplets grow until they are large enough and heavy enough to fall as what you nonscientists would call rain."

"Oh, brother," groaned Sally.

The woman smiled. "Well, that's one way to explain it. You know, you can only learn so much about this world through books. The rest you must learn by going out into the world and living."

"Are you kidding, lady?" Sally laughed. "Fathead here doesn't even like to get out from under his bed!"

Roger got mad and pushed Sally, and Sally pushed him back. That started yet another argument between them.

The woman broke up the fight and told him, "Just as I work in harmony with the Sun, so should you and your sister. It is the only way you will be able to find your parents, Roger."

All around them buds had blossomed into beautiful flowers. The woman looked down at Sally and Roger, now knee deep in dozens of colorful blooms, and smiled at their amazement. She told the children that if they headed further north, they would eventually find the Four Winds and their parents.

"How did you know we were looking for them?" asked Roger.

She told them that she knew everything. Sally and Roger were just little drops of rain in this vast and wonderful world and—

"We get the point," Sally said, trying to be as gracious as she possibly could.

"Thank you," said Roger. Then, following her directions, they headed north, weaving

their way through the flowers, making sure they didn't crush a single one.

Meanwhile, a certain purple blob of goo glided through the jungle in quiet pursuit until it got caught in a summer shower. Then it no longer had to glide along; it began to walk. A little clumsily at first, but it walked just the same. And it was much bigger now, too.

Chapter Five

The lush, damp jungle gave way to cool, green hills dotted with trees. Roger and Sally sat down under a big apple tree to rest. They watched its red and yellow leaves drift and spin in the breeze. Roger looked sad and tired as he munched on the apple he had picked. He was starting to really miss Mom and Dad.

"What's wrong with *you*?" Sally snapped.

"Nothing," answered Roger. "Why, what's *your* problem?"

They both sat there in silence. It grew darker and colder, and they soon nodded off. In their sleep, they cuddled together shivering and wondered if they'd ever see Mom and Dad again.

A cold night breeze whipped past Roger's nose and woke him up. It was dark. Darker than it had ever been before. They were lost in a thick sea of black, studded with twinkling stars. Roger felt like he could just reach up and grab one. He'd bring it home and put it on his dresser. He missed his room.

Sally, now awake, ordered him to quit crowding her. "We might as well get moving. Which way is north again?"

Roger looked around. Far in the distance, he could see the twinkling North Star. Together they walked toward it through the barren expanse. All was silent. No breeze, nothing. The only sound was their own soft footsteps as they trudged through the tall grass. Roger had always been afraid of the dark, but he was especially frightened now since they didn't know where they were going or what was out there. Sally must have sensed his fear and took Roger's hand.

"Big baby," she muttered. "Scared of everything."

After what seemed like hours and hours of walking, dawn finally came. The children reached some jagged rocks and heard the sound of a distant foghorn. They proceeded cautiously. They didn't know what to expect or what they were looking for, either. A low mist covered their feet. It was cool and damp, and as they continued walking it soon engulfed both of them. Sally held Roger's hand tighter now. The foghorn blew again and again, getting louder and louder. They found themselves at the edge of what they could just make out to be a high cliff that gave way to a deep rocky beach, shrouded in thick white fog.

Suddenly, Roger's hand slipped out of Sally's and the mist swallowed him up. Sally heard rocks tumbling and twigs snapping. Then all was quiet again, except for the foghorn.

"Sally!" Roger yelped in a faraway echo.

"Where are you?" Sally pleaded. She couldn't see a thing and was more scared than ever.

"I'm down here. I slipped and fell," he answered.

"Well, I don't see you! Where are you?"

"Follow my voice. But be careful—it's steep," he answered.

Then there was a long silence until, "Marco," Roger faintly cried.

"What?" Sally asked as she gingerly negotiated the rocks.

"Marco. Like Marco Polo. Say Polo," he replied.

"Polo."

"Marco."

"Polo."

Sally slowly made her way down to the beach. The mist seemed to thin out, and she found Roger. He was sitting on a rock holding his knee. He was frightened and hurt. Sally looked relieved to find him. She hugged him and sniffed. "Don't ever do that again, Fathead." Then she hit him.

His knee was scraped pretty badly. Just like the time he had wanted to see a solar eclipse and had slid halfway down the roof of the garage. Sally examined his injury. She untied her favorite blue ribbon from her hair and carefully wrapped it around Roger's knee. Neither of them said a word.

They followed the sound of the foghorn as they climbed over sharp rocks and around huge boulders. Now they could hear something else, too. It sounded like the low murmur of voices. Then—could it be?—the clatter of dishes and the clinking of cutlery. Yes, that had to be it, but *here*?

"One lump or two, dear?" Lady Fog asked.

"One, please," answered Lord Fog.

Sally and Roger were surprised to find an elegantly dressed and extraordinarily well-mannered couple who were at least twenty feet tall, made completely of misty fog, sitting down to afternoon tea.

"Oh, my," Lady Fog exclaimed as she raised her glasses to examine the minute intruders. "How positively improper to call at teatime," she said with a sniff.

"Quite, quite, my dear," commented Lord Fog, "but we mustn't be rude."

He invited Sally and Roger to dine with them. The kids were already hungrily eyeing

the scones, clotted cream, and finger sand-
wiches, and they eagerly accepted. Sally and
Roger proceeded to devour the food in the
most ill-mannered way. The Fogs would have
none of this.

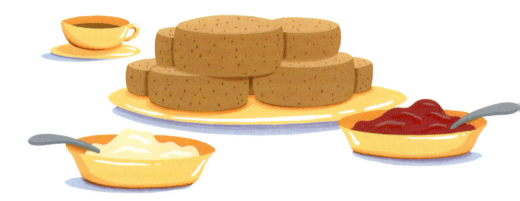

"Ye gods, dear boy, where are your table
manners?" asked Lord Fog in disgust.

They looked up from their plates, faces covered in cream and hands sloppy with butter.

"Sit up straight this instant!" commanded
Lord Fog.

"And elbows off the table!" added Lady Fog.

Sally and Roger obediently snapped to
attention. For the next several hours, Sally

and Roger were given a top-notch education in proper table etiquette. From which utensil to use to never speaking with your mouth full—they learned it all. They were avid students because they were so hungry.

"Lord Fog," asked Roger, only after he had chewed his food thirty-two times and swallowed, "where can we find the Four Winds?"

The lord and lady gave each other a knowing and worried look.

"Why do you wish to find them?" asked Lady Fog.

Sally and Roger explained their predicament and how they had ended up on Fog Beach. "We want to find our parents," said Roger.

"Yeah, we think we miss them," added Sally.

The Fogs directed them north to the Four Winds.

Lady Fog wrapped both Roger and Sally in Lord Fog's best muffler. "It's frightfully cold where you're going," she warned the children.

"Stay bundled up." Roger and Sally bid the Fogs good-bye and thanked them for the scarf and extra scones for the journey.

"Remember your manners!" called Lady Fog as they were swallowed up by the mist and disappeared from sight.

Chapter Six

Tramping over rocks and stones, Sally and Roger made their way north. The pebbles and gravel crunched under their shoes and made their feet hurt. They had never walked this far in all their lives, certainly not on unpaved ground. Roger's arms were sore from carrying the maps, charts, and globe. He asked Sally to carry the globe for a while.

"Forget it! I don't know why you brought that stupid globe anyway!" she said. "Carry it yourself!"

Roger dropped it, and Sally impatiently waited as he chased after it.

Roger thought he heard footsteps. They certainly weren't his, and they sure weren't

Sally's, either. "Did you hear that?" he asked.

"I hope not," said Sally as she started to shiver.

They both turned around to see a large purple figure coming toward them.

Sally and Roger screamed and began to run.

"Behind that rock!" Roger pointed.

They crouched behind a huge boulder.

"What'll we do? It's going to eat us!" Sally exclaimed.

Roger peeked out from behind the rock. Sure enough, there it was. It was sort of running

now and growling, too. It was mad and looked hungry. Roger quickly unwrapped the scarf and put a few stones in it. He stood up and swung the muffler around and around over his head, letting go of one end. A few of the rocks flew over its head, but one got the purple blob right in the eye. Well, it looked like an eye, anyway.

"Rrrroooowwwwwlllll!" it growled as it fell to the ground. It was knocked out cold.

Sally and Roger quickly gathered up their things and hurried away, every once in a while looking over their shoulders.

Chapter Seven

Sally and Roger could barely see as they bent into the driving wind and trudged through knee-deep snow. They were lost. None of the polar bears or penguins were much help at all in giving them directions. On the advice of a walrus, they headed toward the northern lights, the multicolored flashes in the dim distance. Unfortunately, they ran into a bit of a problem—the ocean.

"We never should've listened to that stupid walrus," complained Sally.

"I wrote an essay for science class on walruses," said Roger, "and in all my research, I never read that they had a bad sense of direction."

The piece of ice they were standing on began

to quietly crack and break free of the land.

As darkness fell, Roger explained to Sally that up in the arctic region, depending on the time of year, of course, the days were very short and the nights could last for days.

"Shut up," responded Sally.

By the time they noticed, they had drifted so far from land that the piece of ice now looked like a tiny white sliver in a blue-gray sea. Once again Sally blamed Roger. "This whole thing is your fault, you stupid little fathead!"

"Oh, shut up!" cried Roger. "Why don't you quit complaining and help me figure out what to do!" Sally quietly sat there and stared hopelessly into the icy mist hovering over the deep, dark, freezing ocean. After a while, Roger heard something. It was muffled but distinct. Sally was crying. He walked over to her side of the ice floe not quite knowing what to do. The last time she had cried was when she had lost her pet parakeet, Daphne. She had let it out of its cage to get some exercise and it had flown straight out the window. Sally had waited for days and days, but Daphne never returned. Roger sat down and put his arm around her.

"It's okay, Sally," he said. "We'll find Mom and Dad, I promise."

Sally put her head on Roger's shoulder and cried some more. She eventually fell asleep, warmly snuggled up in the huge scarf. They drifted and drifted. Roger wrapped himself up in the last of the charts and maps and fell

asleep as well. He had many strange dreams as he floated across those dark icy waters. Mermaids sang eerie songs, whales quietly floated by like huge cruise ships, and when he looked up at the stars, they flew away as if they were a flock of birds. But the most vivid dream was of a polar bear in a kayak, silently paddling up to them. He scooped Sally and Roger up and paddled away into the inky night.

Chapter Eight

Roger woke up not knowing whether all that had really happened. He sat up and rubbed his sleepy eyes, but he still couldn't quite figure it out. Sally was stirring something in a massive black pot that hung over a dancing red flame in a huge fireplace. It smelled awfully good, whatever it was. The huge bear in Roger's dream was standing in front of him, smiling.

"It's about time you woke up, Roger," he said.

The figure looking down at Roger was tall yet stout, wore a sealskin parka, and had the widest grin you could possibly fit on a face. And he wasn't a polar bear at all—he was a man.

"Oh, good, you're awake," said Sally, walking up to Roger. "Breakfast is almost ready."

He was still a little confused. Where were they? Who was the man in the parka? Why was Sally cooking? She had never done a bit of work in her life.

They all sat down at a table made of tightly packed snow. In fact, everything in the domed-ceiling room seemed to be made of glistening snow, including the huge fireplace the parka man took the black pot from. But it was still cozy and warm. This didn't make much sense at all.

What smelled so good was a pot of fish soup. Roger hated fish, but perhaps he would eat a little, just to be polite. He tasted some and it was delicious! Sally told the story of their travels—all about the Sun, the rain forest, Fog Beach, the Four Winds, and their parents—right up to the point where they were adrift on the ice floe and cast out to sea.

Sir Snow, the man in the parka, explained that he had been out in his kayak. He had picked them up as they slept and brought them back to his igloo, where they had continued sleeping for almost two days.

"I was checking on some snow I had manufactured. I'm testing a new recipe. Some of my customers have been complaining about the quality of recent snowballs, so I've been experimenting with some new ingredients."

Roger was now more confused than ever. "I thought snow was made by freezing temperatures in the upper region of a cloud that form ice crystals. When water droplets evaporate

and condense on the ice particles, the ice crystals grow rapidly, then fall to earth. If the temperature at the surface of the earth is very low, the ice crystals fall as snow. Scientifically speaking, of course."

Sir Snow laughed. "No, no matter what books say, snow's still made the old-fashioned way. Would you like to see how I do it?"

Roger could hardly contain himself. He managed to enthusiastically nod his head and say, "Yes, I would. Thank you."

They followed Sir Snow down a long, sparkling ice-bricked hallway to an enormous room. It was at least a dozen square miles in size, Roger figured. In the center of it all was what had to be the biggest furnace he had ever seen. Flames—red, purple, green, yellow, and orange—roared inside the opening as tiny overall-clad snowmen shoveled coal into it. As he watched the flickering colors, Roger real- ized these must be the lights the walrus had instructed them to follow. He told Sir Snow that people called them the aurora borealis and thought they were a scientific phenomenon.

"Hmmm. Interesting," Sir Snow said, smiling to himself and chuckling. He led the children over to a conveyor belt that ran from the furnace along the frozen walls of the massive factory. Conveyor belts rose in a spiral, one on top of the other, hundreds of them, maybe, right up to the bluish-white ceiling.

"Every flake of snow I manufacture must be completely unique. Each one is carefully inspected before being approved. You can't imagine how many snowflakes are rejected."

He explained that the duplicate snowflakes were melted down and recycled. Nothing was wasted. Then Sir Snow and Roger engaged in a long discussion about what

could be done to improve the quality of snow for snowball making.

"I thought we were looking for Mom and Dad," said Sally anxiously.

Roger waved her away. "Just a minute," he said.

Roger suggested adding some paste or even sugar. They were white and sticky. This impressed Sir Snow.

"How would you like to stay here and work for me, Roger?" he asked.

Working for Sir Snow would be so much fun and exciting. Roger was about to accept when he looked over at Sally's sad face and said, "I appreciate your offer, but we really need to find the Four Winds."

"And our mom and dad," said Sally. "We miss our parents an awful lot," she added, suddenly sounding sad.

Sir Snow could see how sad they were just by looking at them. He led them to the back door of the factory and outside into the cold, frosty morning. A gigantic bright-red snow-mobile sat half covered under a drift of snow. "I can take you most of the way, but you'll have to walk the last few miles yourselves. But I should warn you two about the Four Winds."

He explained that in his business, he needed the Four Winds to distribute his product. "But I have to keep an eye on them constantly. They're known for being dishonest and sometimes even downright mean."

Sir Snow started to dig out the buried snowmobile. Roger and Sally pitched in and helped uncover it so they could be on their way. Neither Sally nor Roger ever had to shovel the walkway at home. Dad always paid someone to do it. Roger had never realized how much fun it could be.

Soon they were whooshing through the snow at top speed. The twinkling white hills, snow-covered trees, and occasional penguin all whipped by in a blur. They got to where they were going in no time flat.

Chapter Nine

The snowmobile slowed to a stop. The sun was shining, it was a little warmer than before, and the snow on the ground was soft and watery.

"This is as far as I can take you," Sir Snow said. Roger and Sally hopped off the snow-mobile and thanked him again and again. They waved good-bye as he drove away. He waved back and disappeared into the gray sky and white snow. Then all was quiet. Except for one thing. One tiny noise so faint that Sally and Roger didn't even hear it at first. A small echo, really. As they trudged along, that thin little sound grew and grew. It became louder and louder until it made the hair on the back of Roger's neck stand up. They both stopped in their tracks.

"Uh-oh," said Sally as she turned around and saw the purple figure. It was at least fifteen feet tall now. It had arms and the ugliest face you'd ever seen. Roger and Sally ran as fast as they could through the thick snow, but it was no use. There was no way they could outrun the beast.

"Up that hill!" cried Roger to Sally as he hung on to his dented globe and what was left of the tattered maps and charts. Sally did her best to climb the steep hill.

"Hurry!" yelled Roger, poking her in the back, trying to get her to move faster. The purple creature was getting closer.

"Roger! Why are we doing this?"

"Just climb! I have an idea! Hurry!" he shouted.

They finally made it up the hill, and Roger

quickly started to roll a huge snowball.

"Are you nuts?" hollered Sally. "This huge gross pile of glop—that, may I remind you, you created—is about to eat us or something and you're making a snowman?"

"Can't you quit complaining for two seconds and just help me do this?" he cried.

"Okay, okay," she grumbled.

Now the renegade science experiment was climbing the hill. They could see its yellow eye and little spiky teeth. And, oh, that smell. They were doomed for sure.

"Help me push, Sally!" yelled Roger as he nudged the massive snowball over the edge of the hill. They gave it a mighty shove, and down it rolled. That big stinky mess didn't know what hit it.

Down the hill the giant snowball rolled with the creature trapped inside. It came to rest in a huge snowdrift. Sally stood there, silently blinking, her nose running. With a huge grin on his face, Roger proudly stood on top of the

hill, wind blowing through his hair, with his hands on his hips.

"Nuts, huh?" he said.

Even Sally had to admit, her brother may have been weird, but he sure was smart. She didn't say a word as she carried his globe down the other side of the hill.

Chapter Ten

As they trotted along, Roger beamed. He held his head high and grinned to himself. For once, Sally couldn't call him a fathead. The Sun was peeking out from behind the clouds in a crisp blue sky. The distant sound of birds chirping could be heard. Roger started to whistle along with them but suddenly grew cold and silent as a massive shadow fell upon them. They turned around and looked up.

Rrrrrroooaaarrrr! They both turned white and froze. It was back. Big and purple and angrier than ever.

Rrrrroooaaarrr! It growled once again, its yellow eye flashing and ugly teeth gnashing.

Roger fainted.

When he came to, he was alone. Sally was gone. Either the creature had carried her away or it had just eaten her up right on the spot. All Roger had was a path of crooked footprints to follow. He brushed himself off and followed the twisted trail, with that rancid, rotten-egg smell still hanging in the air. He slogged through the soupy, slushy snow until he came to green grass and bluer skies. By this time, Roger had discarded Lord and Lady Fog's huge muffler. The end of the snow was also the end of the trail.

"I guess I should just keep walking in this direction," Roger said to himself, and continued to a cluster of trees atop a small hill. As he made his way through the trees, he heard a faint cry.

"Help! Help me, please," said a small voice.

Roger looked up but could see nothing.

"Oh, please help me out of here!" cried the little voice again.

This time he spotted it. There was a small cloud caught in the branches of a tall tree. It wiggled and twisted but couldn't get free.

"Don't worry," called Roger. "I'll help you!"

Roger quickly climbed up the tree, only slipping once. He was surprised at how easy it was since he had never climbed one before. He climbed out to the branch where the cloud was caught. He shook the branch so hard that the cloud was set free, but he lost his balance and slipped off in the process. The cloud swooped down, and Roger

70

landed on its soft white fluffiness. It gently set Roger down on the ground.

"Thank you, thank you very much," said Roger.

"No, thank *you*. I was caught in that tree for over an hour, and I didn't think I'd ever get free."

Roger told the little cloud he needed to find his sister, Sally. "There aren't any more footprints for me to follow," said Roger, "only that awful smell."

The little cloud suggested Roger climb on his back and from high up in the sky, they could look for his sister. Up, up, up they went. Roger had never been up so high in all his life. He was up even higher than when his dad had brought him to the office and they'd looked out over the city for miles and miles.

The nasty stench crept into Roger's nose. "That way!" he cried as he pointed to a cluster of jagged, rocky hills. They soon landed safely on a small plateau and Roger sniffed

the air. He followed the odor to an opening in the side of the hill.

"You'd better stay out here. I'll be right back—I hope," said Roger to the little cloud.

Alone, Roger silently crept in. He could hear a voice echoing through the cave and smell a stench like stinky feet. He wound his way through a maze of dark passages, slipping on purple goo once or twice, until he came to a ledge on the cave wall. The voice was becoming quite clear.

"Listen, you big ugly sack of glop, you'll be sorry if you eat me!"

It was Sally all right. She was okay—for the moment, anyway. Roger gave a sigh of relief. He inched closer, being sure to keep himself hidden behind a huge boulder on the ledge. He took a quick glimpse from behind the rock and saw Sally tied to a stalagmite. The purple monster was rubbing two sticks together trying to start a fire, possibly to cook Sally.

Gee, thought Roger, *this thing is smarter than I thought! I must have a plan. It must be clever and ingenious. Hmmm, maybe if I build a crude lever system out of rocks and sticks, I could—*

Suddenly, Roger's globe rolled out of his hand off the ledge he was hiding on. He tried to grab it but he rolled off the ledge as well. Roger landed right in front of the purple beast. It looked down at him, purple drool dripping from his ugly mouth.

"Roger!" cried Sally. "Get me out of here!"

As Roger looked up at the creature, its yellow eye narrowed and it gave a low, hungry growl.

"Do something, Roger!" screamed Sally. "Don't just sit there!"

His mind raced. He had no plan. He had nothing. Nothing at all. The monster licked its thin lips. Moving toward Roger, it opened its mouth wide. Roger backed up as much as he could, and his hand touched something round. Before he knew it, Roger was flinging the globe into the creature's big mouth. Bull's-eye!

"Aaak!" it croaked. The monster's slimy hands clutched at its throat as the globe stuck in its mouth. Not bad for a kid who was always picked last in gym class.

The monster turned a deeper shade of purple, then fell over. It was dead as a doornail. Just to make sure, Roger poked it with a stick.

"I told you we needed the globe," said Roger.

He untied Sally, and as they made their way to the opening of the cave she turned to Roger. "You know, if you weren't my brother, I'd say you were a pretty brave guy," she said, hugging him.

Outside, Roger introduced Sally to the little cloud. The children explained to him that they needed to find their parents, but when they mentioned the Four Winds the cloud looked frightened and even a little more white than before.

"You'll have to talk to my mom and dad. I'm not allowed to go near where they live by myself," explained the little cloud.

Sally and Roger hopped on his back and they floated up into the sky. Up and up they went into a layer of white mist.

"Who have we here?" asked Mama Cloud.

The little cloud introduced Sally and Roger to his parents and told them where they wanted to go.

"*Hmmmm,*" said Papa Cloud, "are you sure you want to go *there?*"

Mama Cloud looked terribly worried. "That's no place for children," she said.

"But Mama," said the little cloud, "the Four Winds have their mother and father. They have to go."

The Clouds agreed. They had to help bring Roger and Sally back together with their parents. After a discussion, they decided to wait until dark and then bring Sally and Roger to where the Four Winds lived.

Chapter Eleven

The sky turned from pale blue to bright peach and then to deep purple. Sally, Roger, and the Clouds silently floated down to the edge of a dark, barren expanse of flat, dusty land. Off in the distance, they could just make out a dilapidated old house with dim lights flickering in the windows.

"That's where they live," whispered Papa Cloud. "We would come with you if we could, but the Four Winds would blow us apart forever if we went near them."

"Oh, do be careful," pleaded Mama Cloud.

"You can do it," said the little cloud as Roger and Sally shook his fluffy hand. "Good luck," he said.

Sally and Roger gratefully thanked the

Clouds for all their help. As the Clouds floated away, Sally and Roger slowly walked hand in hand across the great stretch of land under a deep dark sky. They could hear the whistle and drone of the wind wheezing through the broken-down house. Their hearts beat faster as they put their feet on the first creaky step of the porch. The old house shook and rattled as the wind whipped through it. They could hear deep low laughter and high screeching cackles.

As they approached the door, it blew open with a bang. A strong gust made Sally and Roger a little unsteady, but they bent into the wind and walked inside. The house was huge. They could barely see the ceiling, it was so high. And, boy, was it a mess. Dust, garbage, and newspapers all flew about in little tornadoes around the room.

There they were—Mom and Dad, slaves to the Four Winds. Mom, weary and tousled, was rushing about trying to clean and dust, but the winds kept creating more and more of

a mess. Dad was busy serving them massive plates of food and still they demanded more.

"Faster! Faster! You lazy louts! No wonder your children didn't want you!" cackled the fat one. All the Four Winds laughed and blew Mom and Dad twirling up to the ceiling.

"Well, well, well. We've been expecting you. What took you so long?" said the ugly Wind sibling, spotting Roger and Sally. He laughed and blew a cold wind right in their faces, shutting the door.

"Mom! Dad!" cried Roger.

"Roger!" cried Dad. "You and Sally get out of here! They'll hurt you!"

And with that, one of the Four Winds, fatter and uglier than the first two, blew a gust of wind at Dad that sent him even higher, spinning in a hurricane of trash and garbage. The big one picked up Roger and said, "You must be Roger, the rotten little kid who didn't want his parents anymore! Don't worry, Junior, we put them to good use!"

"Leave my children alone!" cried Mom as she tried to fight her way down to Sally and Roger from up near the ceiling.

"Why don't you let them go, you big bag of hot air!" yelled Sally.

"You must be the spoiled sister! I hear you're worse than the little fathead here!" He picked up Sally.

"Let her go!" cried Roger, swinging his fists.

The Winds laughed so hard, the walls shook. They blew a mighty gust of wind at Roger and Sally, who flew up to the ceiling where Mom and Dad still were. They were all floating and spinning within their own little tornadoes.

"Roger!" cried Dad as the financial section of a newspaper stuck to his head. "What are you and Sally doing here?"

"We came to rescue you, Dad!" hollered Roger.

"Sally! Roger! You shouldn't have come!" yelled Mom over the driving wind. She was floating in a swirl of old magazines, left shoes, and broken kitchen appliances.

"Bob!" she called to Dad. "Do something!"

Dad was having his own problems trying to fight off bits of computer equipment and wires tangled around his legs. Sally was struggling with the bow on an old pink party dress that kept getting stuck in her mouth.

"*Ppttuuu—*" spat Sally.

Mom and Dad were exhausted. Sally was dizzy and scared. So was Roger, but he fought his way back down to the Four Winds, who were now all doubled up with laughter. "Let my parents go, you big goons," demanded Roger. They all laughed harder, and one of them said, "Fat chance, pip-squeak. Button your lip or I'll knock you into next week."

"I—I'm not afraid of you!" yelled Roger as he tried to fight off the driving wind.

"Oh, yeah?" asked the biggest one. All four winds inhaled. They blew gale winds and storms, they threw balls of lightning right at him, and claps of thunder cracked and exploded over his head. Roger fought and fought. He clenched his teeth and fists and struggled to keep his balance. The Winds laughed and laughed. Then a hurricane blast sent Roger flying back up to the ceiling.

Sally caught Roger's hand. Roger, Sally, Mom, and Dad were all floating and spinning in the center of one big tornado. Hand in hand, Roger and Sally began to sink toward the floor. It seemed that once they were holding hands the Winds had to blow twice as hard to keep Roger and Sally up there.

Roger realized this and called, "Mom! Dad! Take our hands!" Roger reached out to them. Mom and Dad fought their way down to Roger and Sally, who were still sinking. Finally,

Mom, Dad, Sally, and Roger were all holding hands in a circle. They gently floated down to the floor even though the Four Winds tried as hard as they could to blast them apart. As the family touched down on the floor, the Winds collapsed in a heap in the corner, exhausted and panting. The family, still holding hands, ran as fast as they could through the front door and down the steps.

Roger, Sally, Mom, and Dad frantically ran across the rough and rocky ground, stumbling and helping each other up along the way.

They soon came to an old twisted dead tree far from the Four Winds' shack. Dad decided that they should take a rest under it. Mom hugged Sally and covered Roger's face with kisses. For once he didn't say, "Quit it, Mom!" but hugged her right back. Dad joined in, too. No one came out and said it, but they sure were glad to be together again.

Mom fretted over every bruise and scratch on the two kids. Dad scolded Roger and Sally for coming to get them. "There's no knowing what could've happened to you two!" But then he hugged them again anyway.

"We're okay, Dad," said Sally.

"Yeah, you and Mom were worth it!" said Roger.

Dad smiled as he helped them up. "Thank you, Roger. Thank you, Sally."

"No problem." Roger smiled.

Mom stood up, wiped her eyes, and said "All right, Roger. Now which way is home?"

He looked at the black night sky for a clue but found nothing. "I'm not sure. . . ."

"Need some help?" asked a voice from high above. The Cloud family gently floated down and silently landed in front of Roger and his family.

"I guess everything turned out okay," said the little cloud as he and Roger shook hands.

"Mom, Dad, this is the Cloud family. They helped us find you."

Dad asked Papa Cloud how to get home. Papa Cloud suggested that Roger and his family hop up on the Clouds and they'd float them all the way home.

Up they hopped and off they went. They leisurely floated through the night, passing rocky hills then green fields. Soon the Sun

keep a kite up in the air. Sally was talking to Mom, and Mom was actually barbecuing. All right, so it was tofu, but it was a start. As Roger ran to try to make the kite fly, he accidentally knocked down Sally, who fell into the bushes.

"You stupid fathead!" she yelled, then sat there for a few seconds, realized how silly she looked, and started to laugh. Roger helped her up, and they managed to get the kite to stay up in the air and even do a few tricks.

There were no phone calls, tennis lessons, cocktail parties, or television. Roger was happy. Happier than he had been in a long time.